SAMURAI JACK™

Mountain of Mayhem

by Tracey West

Based on "Samurai Jack," as created by Genndy Tartakovsky

Scholastic Inc.

New York   Toronto   London   Auckland   Sydney

Mexico City   New Delhi   Hong Kong   Buenos Aires

No part of this publication may be reproduced in whole or in part, or stored in a retrieval system, or transmitted in any form or by any means, electronic, mechanical, photocopying, recording, or otherwise, without written permission of the publisher. For information regarding permission, write to Scholastic Inc., Attention: Permissions Department, 557 Broadway, New York, NY 10012.

ISBN 0-439-40975-6

Cover and interior illustrations by Ken Edwards

Designed by Carisa Swenson

12 11 10 9 8 7 6 5 4 3 2 1   2 3 4 5 6 7/0

Printed in the U.S.A.

First printing, November 2002

"*There is one who can help you with your quest. A wise man, a sage. He has the knowledge to send you back to your time.*"

The monks' words echoed in Samurai Jack's mind as he took step after step across the wide, barren valley. The monks had told him about the sage over a meal of coarse bread and strong tea. Jack had accepted the news — and the food — gratefully.

Finding the monks hadn't been easy. His journey began with a farmer, who told him a troupe of wandering musicians might have the knowledge he needed. The musicians had sent him to a fisherman. And the fisherman told him to find an old woman who lived deep in the Dark Woods.

The old woman had sent him to the monks. For the first time in weeks, Jack had felt an unfamiliar feeling — hope.

Hope was something in short supply in this world, thanks to Aku. Ages ago, Jack had fought the evil shape-shifter in a desperate attempt to stop him from ravaging his homeland. After a fierce battle, Aku sent the samurai warrior far into the future. When Jack arrived, the world was a sad and evil place. All those who opposed Aku had either been destroyed or lived in fear of his wrath.

Jack knew there was only one way to undo Aku's evil. He had to find a way to travel back to the past and destroy Aku before he was able to take over the world.

That goal is what had led him to the monks.

"Our ancient books speak of a warrior who will deliver the world from Aku," said the eldest monk. Bright green eyes peered out from her wrinkled face. Soft fuzz covered her shaved head.

"Many years ago, one of our order began a study of great magicks," she went on. "He was determined to find a way for this great warrior to go back through time, so Aku could be destroyed before the world fell under his evil rule. He spent decades alone on the Shen Mountains. The last time we spoke to him, he told us he had succeeded. Now he waits for the great avenger to find him."

Jack swallowed his tea. "Where is he now?" he asked.

The monk looked him directly in the eyes. "He lives alone. On the other side of the Shen Mountain range."

Jack set down the carved mug that held his tea. This was not welcome news. Jack knew of the Shen Mountains. The range stretched out for so many miles that it took months to travel from beginning to end. Jack had heard that there was once a tunnel that went under the mountains, but it had collapsed long ago.

The best way to reach the sage would be to climb over the mountains. It meant many days of difficult climbing, but it was the fastest and surest way to go. Jack knew it was the path he must take.

"Thank you," Jack told the monks. He stood up.

The elderly monk waved her hand, and two younger monks appeared. One gave Jack a small package wrapped in paper.

"Bread for your journey," the eldest monk explained. "You will need strength to cross the Shen Mountains."

The second monk held a cord with a small

talisman on the end. Carved into it was a bird — a raven, Jack thought.

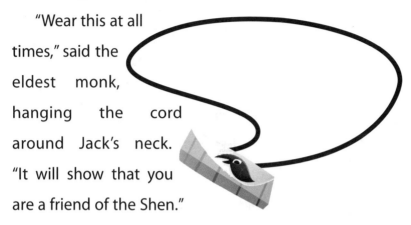

"Wear this at all times," said the eldest monk, hanging the cord around Jack's neck. "It will show that you are a friend of the Shen."

Jack raised an eyebrow. The monk looked startled.

"Surely the great warrior has heard of the Shen?" she asked.

Jack shook his head.

"Then it will do you well to hear it," she said. "The Shen are the ancient spirits who inhabit the mountain pass. If you are a friend, they will help you. If you are not, then you will never find your way out of the mountains."

Jack nodded and thanked the monks again. Then he started his journey toward the mountain range.

After three days of traveling, Jack's meeting with the monks seemed far away. So did the meal. He satisfied his hunger with the meager plant life he found in the valley. He did not touch the bread. Looking up at the jagged mountain peaks, he knew he would need it later.

It was late afternoon when Jack reached the foothills of the mountain. Another person might have waited until morning to begin the climb, but not Jack. His years of samurai training had taught him to see in the dark as easily as a cat — and to step just as lightly.

The sun set as Jack climbed. A purple glow shone on the mountain peaks. Jack stopped to admire the sight. He rested, ate a bit of the bread, and then moved on.

Jack first noticed the fog as it swirled around his feet. The moist, gray mist slowly snaked up around him. As Jack walked on, the fog became thicker and thicker. He held his hand out in front of him, and it disappeared from sight.

Jack stopped. His eyes could no longer guide him. But his ears could hear the rustle of a leaf or the sound of a

tiny pebble tumbling down the path. His feet could sense if the ground underneath was rocky or smooth. Using the rest of his senses, he cautiously made his way forward.

Up and up Jack climbed. Soon he stopped again. Something did not feel right. His feet, his nose, his ears — what they told him did not make sense.

He had been traveling in circles. He was almost sure of it.

Jack tried again —

and stopped again. He was positive. He should have been going up, but instead he was going around and around. It was impossible.

Jack frowned. It wasn't like him to become disoriented. He closed his eyes and tried to focus.

Jack turned slowly to the right. He opened his eyes. He took one long step . . .

. . . and plunged right off of the mountain!

2

S everal things happened next, all within one second. Jack drew his sword and thrust it into the side of the mountain.

The cord around Jack's neck swung right into the sword's path. The sword cleanly sliced through the cord.

Jack clutched the sword's handle with both hands. He was safe, but not out of danger. Beneath him, he heard the sound of the lost talisman as it clattered down the mountainside.

But Jack had bigger worries now. With one arm, he reached up until he touched flat ground. He pulled himself to safety, then reached down and pulled out his sword.

Jack sat on the ground and thought. The thick, damp fog had settled on the mountain like a blanket. He could not trust his senses in this fog. Something — or some-one — was toying with him.

There was nothing he could do but wait.

For a time, the only sound Jack heard was his own steady breathing.

And then . . . the flutter of wings. A bird had landed at his feet.

The bird's bright green eyes shone through the fog. They reminded Jack of the elderly monk in the valley.

The bird stepped closer. Black feathers gleamed on its body. Its thick, black beak curved downward.

A raven.

The raven cocked its head to one side. "Not many come through these mountains," he said in a scratchy voice. "Are you friend or enemy?"

The fact that the raven was talking did not surprise Jack. He had long ago learned not to be surprised about anything in Aku's world.

"I am friend to those who fight the demon Aku," Jack answered, "and enemy to those who aid him."

"We will see," said the raven, hopping around on his gnarled black feet. "Maybe you lie to us? *Craawk!*"

"I do not lie," Jack said simply.

The raven did not seem impressed. He hopped up and perched on Jack's shoulder. "You may be friend," he said. "But right now you are lost. I can help you, but you must follow me!"

Jack thought about this. "How do I know that *you* are a friend?"

"*Caaaw!*" the raven cackled. It almost sounded like he was laughing. "You shall see."

Jack knew that he might never be able to pass through the strange fog on his own. The raven's help might be his only hope. Then again, it was suspicious that the raven showed up when he did. He could be leading Jack into some kind of trap.

But a samurai warrior was not afraid of danger. And following the raven was better than sitting in the fog forever.

"I will follow you," Jack said.

The raven's head bobbed up and down. "Good!" he said. "Now stand up and hold out your arm."

Jack did as he was told, and the raven climbed down to Jack's fist.

"Forward!" the raven cried.

The raven called out instructions, leading Jack farther and farther through the fog. Jack could sense that the raven was indeed leading them on a sure path. He wasn't going around in circles anymore.

They walked on and on. The fog began to thin, and soon Jack could see stars shining brightly in the black sky above.

"*Caaaw!* Just a little farther," the raven instructed. Soon they arrived at a small, flat area just off of the path. A small stream of clear water trickled past them.

The raven fluttered its wings and flew to a tall rock.

"Time to stop!" the raven said.

Something in Jack wanted to keep going, but it did

look like a good place to stop. He knelt down and took a drink of the water.

"Thank you for your help," he told the raven.

"We will see," the raven replied. Then he tucked his head underneath his wing and began to snore.

Jack stretched out on the dusty ground and stared at the stars. Aku had changed many things in the world, but the stars were just the same. The thought comforted him as he drifted off to sleep.

The raven's voice echoed in Jack's head as he slept, tossing and turning.

Friend or enemy?

Friend or enemy?

We shall see . . .

Then the raven's voice became many voices. The voices became louder . . . and changed.

They no longer sounded like the coarse croaking of the raven. Now they were light and eerie, like the sound of chimes on a windy day.

We shall see . . .

We shall see . . .

PROVE YOURSELF, JACK!

Jack woke with a start.

The raven was gone. But instead, three ghostly apparitions floated in front of him.

3

Jack stared at the apparitions, his hand on his sword. The three figures seemed to be made out of mist. Jack could see the stars shining right through them.

Each figure was a different color. One, a shimmering blue, looked like a beautiful woman with long hair. The second was gold and looked like a small child. The third figure was green and appeared to be an old man.

Jack realized he wasn't exactly sure what they looked like. As they floated in the air in front of him, their faces and bodies seemed to be constantly shifting. First the gold figure had the sweet face of a little boy, and in the next second it had the nose and whiskers of a cat.

"We are the Shen," the three figures repeated.

Jack waited a minute before answering. Once again,

he could not trust his senses. He would have to trust his instincts instead. Were the Shen servants of Aku?

No, he finally decided. The monks would have warned him of that. However, the Shen might still be dangerous. The monks had given him the talisman to protect him —

but that was long gone. He would have to proceed with care.

"I am Jack," he said finally. Then he realized they had already called him by his name.

The spirits laughed, and it reminded him of the sound of small bells ringing. They danced in the air around Jack, trailing streaks of blue, green, and gold light behind them. Their bodies were translucent, glowing with light.

"Why are you sleeping, Jack?" asked the boy.

"There is no time to waste," said the woman.

"Hurry, Jack. Hurry!" cried the old man.

Jack felt a cold breeze as the Shen flew around his body.

"I am looking for a sage who lives on the other side of the mountains," Jack said. "The monks told me that he once lived among you."

The Shen swirled around him, faster and faster.

"Are you worthy, Jack?"

"Are you friend?"

"Are you enemy?"

Jack was getting tired of that question.

"On my honor," Jack said. "I am an enemy only to Aku."

In an instant, the Shen stopped their whirling and lined up in front of Jack. The woman floated between the old man and the boy.

"Follow us," she said.

The Shen were playing a game with him. The raven was part of it, he knew. But it seemed that he would not get over the mountain unless he played along. He remembered the words of the monk: *"If you are a friend, they will help you. If you are not, then you will never find your way out of the mountains."*

Jack stood up.

The three spirits smiled. Jack followed as they floated away from him and headed up a trail along the stream.

The morning sun was just beginning to brighten the dark sky. Jack realized he must have slept longer than he thought. He hoped the sun would take away the chill that had crept into his bones.

But the sun never seemed to make it any higher in

the sky. Jack walked on and on in the dim light. He wasn't sure if they were making any progress. The path took them down a steep hill, and then back up again. Up and down they went. The Shen did not speak at all, and Jack did not ask any questions.

After a while, a light rain began to fall. Jack wasn't sure if it was hours or minutes after they had started. Time did not seem to exist when you were around the Shen.

The rain began to fall harder. The Shen stopped in front of a dark, small cave opening.

"Shelter," said the young boy.

Jack nodded. Ordinarily, a little rain would not stop him. But he was not making the rules here — the Shen were.

The Shen disappeared inside the cave. Jack followed, but they were nowhere to be seen.

Jack turned around. There was nothing but solid rock where the cave entrance used to be.

"Good-bye, Jack!" he heard the Shen say from outside of the cave. Then he heard their laughter.

And then there was silence.

The Shen had trapped him.

Jack's eyes adjusted to the darkness. He felt along the wall where the entrance had been. It was completely smooth. The Shen had not just blocked the entrance, but they had used strong magic to seal it closed.

Jack examined the rest of his surroundings. The opposite cave wall opened up into some kind of tunnel. That was good. The tunnel might lead to a way out. At least it was an option.

Jack slowly made his way through the tunnel. His sandals made no sound as he walked across the hard rock. The only thing Jack could hear was the steady sound of his own breathing. Until . . .

Plink!

Jack stopped.

Plink!

Two small, round rocks rolled by his feet.

Plink!

Another rock struck Jack just below his knee.

Plink! Plink! Plink!

Jack dodged one flying rock after another. Under his breath, he uttered an oath.

The Shen had led him into an ambush!

Jack's heart raced as he zigzagged along the tunnel, dodging the rocks as he ran. Every step gave him more energy. The fog, the spirits — they had made him uneasy. But rocks? He knew how to defend himself against rocks.

By now Jack's eyes had adjusted, and he could see as clearly as if it were daylight. The tunnel opened up into a larger cave. The rocks were being hurled at him from a ledge on the far wall. He couldn't see his attackers. He guessed they were crouched behind the small boulders that lined the ledge.

Jack jumped into the cave, somersaulted, and landed

behind a tall rock on the ground. He crouched down and surveyed the scene.

Plink! Plink! Plink! The small rocks bounced off of the rock in front of him.

And that's when it dawned on Jack. He was being bombarded with small rocks. Pebbles. Not flaming arrows, not poisonous spears, but pebbles. They didn't even hurt when they hit him.

Jack peered out from behind the rock protecting him and eyed the ledge. A small creature — no taller than Jack's waist — popped up from behind a boulder and hurled a rock at Jack.

Jack stood up and caught the rock in his hand.

"I am not here to hurt you," he called out. "I am lost."

Jack heard the sound of whispering voices on the ledge. One of the creatures stepped out into Jack's sight.

"We have many rocks," the creature said in a shaking voice. "We're not afraid to throw them all."

Jack studied the creature. It walked on two legs and had a body that looked much like a human's. But it was covered in smooth white skin that glowed softly in the dark. There wasn't any hair on the creature's body, or any clothing, either. It stared at Jack with two large, dark eyes.

"I will not hurt you," Jack repeated. "I need your help."

The creature ducked behind the boulder. There was more whispering. Then the creature reappeared.

"We will take you to our leader," the creature said.

Three more creatures walked out from behind the boulders. They looked almost identical, and were all carrying heavy-looking sacks.

"We have many rocks," said another creature. This one looked a little smaller than the others. "So don't try anything."

Jack nodded. The creatures walked down to where Jack was standing. He noticed that they strained as they dragged the bags behind them.

"I am Jack," he said.

The one who seemed to be the leader stepped forward. "I am Tock," he said. "You can march with me. The others will follow."

"We are watching you!" said the shorter one.

Jack held back a smile. These creatures were small and weak, and they had useless weapons. But they were brave. He appreciated that.

Tock led the group through another tunnel. This one seemed to lead down toward the center of the mountain. The wall was so low in places that Jack had to stoop over as he walked.

"If you truly do come in peace, then I apologize for attacking you," Tock said as they walked. "Our people, the Terras, have lived in these mountains for many years. We were never disturbed — until a few months ago. An evil has come to this mountain." Tock coughed and wheezed as he spoke. It seemed difficult for him to breathe.

Tock's words saddened Jack. There seemed to be no escape from evil in Aku's world.

Behind him, Jack could hear the other Terras strain-ing as they carried their burdens. Jack stopped. He turned around and silently took the sacks from each one. They looked relieved.  Tock, on the other hand, looked mildly alarmed.

Without a word, Jack slung the sacks over his shoul-ders and kept going. Tock seemed to relax.

Before long the tunnel opened up in front of them. Jack ducked and followed Tock into another cavern.

Jack froze. The sight before him was more beautiful than anything he had seen in a long while. The huge cave was the size of a small city. Jack counted four levels from the floor to the ceiling.

Crystal stalactites hung from the ceiling. Some were twice the size of Jack, while others were no taller than Tock's head. The thousands of stalactites glowed with the soft light coming from the bodies of hundreds of Terras as they moved about the levels.

Jack followed Tock to the bottom level. From there they walked to the center of the cavern. One of the Terras sat atop a tall throne made of smooth, polished stone.

Tock bowed low before the Terra.

"We found this stranger in the outer passages," Tock said, rising. "He says he is lost. He needs our help."

"But if he's lying we will throw more rocks at him!" said the smaller Terra.

The leader of the Terras stared at Jack's face for several moments. Then he let out a long sigh.

"We would help you if we could, stranger," he said in a sad voice. "But right now we can help no one."

The leader paused, gazed up at the stalactites, and then looked at Jack again.

"Our people are dying."

Tock looked agitated. "Respectfully, Grotto," he said, bowing again. "We do not know that we are dying. Such talk makes our people give up hope."

Grotto shook his head. "We will not live long without clean water, Tock," he said. "You know that."

Grotto turned to Jack. "Something is infecting the underground spring that supplies our water," he explained. "Our people have been sickly for weeks. Even you cannot deny that, Tock."

"Then let us go to the source of the spring," Tock said. "We can find what is causing the infection and put an end to it. My men and I will go."

A crowd of Terras was beginning to form around Grotto's throne. Many of them stared at Jack, the first stranger they had seen in their lives. Others watched Tock and Grotto carefully. Jack guessed they had heard this argument before.

"You would not survive," Grotto said.

"Then that is our choice," Tock said. Once again Jack admired his bravery.

Jack stepped forward. "I will go," he said.

Grotto smiled for the first time. "Brave words, stranger. But I thought it was *you* who needed *our* help."

"I need to find a way out of the mountains," Jack

replied. "If you know a way, you can help me. But first I will help you."

"And I will go with him," Tock said.

"And I will go too," said the smaller Terra, stepping forward.

A cheer went up from the crowd of Terras — followed by coughs and wheezes.

"I see I cannot stop you," Grotto said. "Very well, then. You three shall go. But first, you must eat with us."

Jack's stomach rumbled in thanks. The last thing he had eaten was some of the monk's bread, and that was a long time ago.

Minutes later, Jack was seated at a stone table with Grotto, Tock, and the rock-throwing Terra, who was called Micah. The table was in a stone chamber with a low ceiling. What seemed like an army of Terras scurried around the table, piling plates of food around him.

Jack looked down hungrily at his plate. Staring back at him was a large insect with too many legs to count. Thick worms made a circle around the edge of the stone plate.

Grotto beamed at Jack. "Only the finest food for our guests!" he said proudly.

Grotto, Tock, and Micah began to shovel the worms into their mouths. Jack closed his eyes and tried to pretend it was sushi. He could use the protein, anyway.

A Terra servant put a goblet in front of him. Inside the goblet he poured a thick, pea-green liquid.

"The juice of the lambada slug," Tock explained. "It's the only thing safe to drink anymore."

Insect protein was one thing, but slug juice was another. Jack reached for the flask that he carried around his waist. He had filled it with fresh water from the clean mountain stream.

"You have shared your food with me," he said. "Let me share my water with you."

The Terras's eyes got bigger, if that was possible. Grotto snapped his fingers, and new goblets appeared. Jack filled them all until the flask was empty.

"Don't worry," Micah said as he gulped down the water. "We'll pack plenty of lambada juice for our journey."

Somehow, Jack did not feel relieved.

"The time of resting comes in a few hours," Tock said when they were finished eating. "We should be able to go a good distance before then."

Jack guessed that "the time of resting" was what the Terras considered nighttime. With no way to see the sky, night or day meant nothing to them — just sleeping and not sleeping.

"I am ready," Jack said.

The Terra servants gave them each a pack of food and supplies. Micah's pack looked suspiciously heavy.

"Extra rocks," he explained. "Just in case."

Tock and Micah said good-bye to their loved ones. Then Jack, Tock, and Micah began their journey.

They started through a dark tunnel that led out of the first level of Terra. Tock held a map made of flimsy green paper.

"The founders of Terra mapped all of the outer passages long ago," Tock explained as they walked. "This map will show us how to find the source of our spring."

"Grotto spoke of many dangers on this path," Jack said. "Do you know what they are?" Jack had had enough surprises over the last few days.

Tock stopped. "Well, to begin with, there's this one," he said.

The path ended abruptly. In front of them was a gaping chasm. There was at least twenty feet of emptiness before the path continued on the other side.

No, not emptiness exactly. Jack peered down to see red-orange flames leaping up toward them. Standing between them and the rest of their journey was a flaming pit of fire.

"I see," Jack said.

"Maybe we can throw rocks at it," Micah suggested. "Don't be a rock head, Micah," Tock said. "We jump over it, right, Jack?"

Jack surveyed the fire pit. One minute the flames would leap high, and the next, they would recede, like ocean waves hitting the beach. If he timed the jump correctly, he could get across while the flames were low. He could make it.

Tock and Micah, on the other hand, would never make it all the way across on their own. Jack crouched down in front of Micah.

"Climb on," he said.

"You're going to carry us across?" Micah asked. "No way. I am a Terra. I can do it myself. Right, Tock?"

The look on Tock's face showed that he could see Jack's point of view.

"A leader does not let his men take foolish risks," Jack said.

Tock nodded. "Jack's right. Go with him, Micah. We'll need your strength for the dangers ahead."

"I will come back for you," Jack told Tock.

Jack hoisted Micah onto his back. The little Terra stubbornly clung to his sack of rocks, but the extra weight did not bother Jack. He stared at the fire pit.

The red-hot flames leaped high, touching the top of the tunnel. Then they began to recede.

Jack took a running start. He ran to the edge of the chasm and jumped.

Jack could feel the searing heat of the flames below him, but he kept his eyes focused on his goal. He landed on the other side just as the flames shot up again.

"We did it!" Micah cheered.

Jack knelt down, and Micah climbed off of his back. Jack stood up and faced the fire pit again. The flames shot up, and Jack sprang into the air.

Jack sailed over the flames as they receded once again. Dust kicked up underneath his sandals as he landed safely on the other side.

"How do you do that?" Tock asked, a look of wonder on his face.

Jack didn't answer. He knelt down again, and Tock climbed on his back.

Jack straightened and watched the rhythm of the flames. Up, then down. Up, then down. Up, then . . . jump!

Jack sailed across the cavern with Tock on his back. The flames slowly receded beneath them — and then shot back up unexpectedly.

"Jack!" Tock cried as a stray flame licked at his legs. Tock released his grip around Jack's neck and began slapping at the flame with his right arm.

The sudden movement shifted Jack's balance. They

were speeding toward the other side of the chasm, and Jack could tell they were not going to make it.

"Hold on!" Jack cried.

Jack reached out and grabbed onto the edge of the rock outcrop with both arms. The rest of his body slammed into a wall of rock. He could feel Tock lose his balance and slide down his back.

Tock managed to grab ahold of Jack's ankles just in time. The samurai and the Terra dangled above the fire pit. The flames had lowered again, but they could shoot back up at any second.

"Tock, climb!" Micah called from above.

Tock quickly scrambled up Jack's body, stood on Jack's head, and climbed onto the outcrop. Then Jack pulled himself over the outcrop just as the flames shot up again. The hot fire licked at his sandals as he made his way to safety.

"Sorry, Jack," Tock said, shaken.

Jack stood up and straightened his robe.

"We are all right," he said. "Let's keep going."

"Right," Tock said. He took out the map again. Then he led the way into a new tunnel.

The three companions didn't say anything for a long time. Tock finally broke the silence.

"Grotto was right," he said. "We never could have made this journey on our own. You saved us, Jack."

Jack didn't answer. Tock continued.

"You see, there has never been an army in Terra," Tock explained. "We didn't need one. We have lived alone inside the mountain for ages. No one has ever bothered us. But not long ago the scouts on the outer passages reported intruders in the mountain."

"That is when our water became poisoned," Micah added.

"It was my idea to start an army so we could protect ourselves," Tock said. "But we have no training, no weapons."

"We have rocks!" Micah said.

"Yes," Tock said, sighing. "We have rocks."

Jack had seen this before. Peaceful people forced to defend themselves against Aku's evil. It was never easy.

They walked on and on. They passed insects scuttling along the tunnel floor. They passed spiders spinning webs along the walls. But there was no sign of any danger. From time to time Micah passed a vial of lambada juice among them. Jack managed to choke some down.

Tock finally stopped. "The time of resting is long past," he said. "We can sleep here."

"I'll take the first watch," Micah said.

Jack started to protest, but Tock stopped him. "Rest, Jack," Tock said. "We owe you one."

Jack did not want to hurt the Terras' pride. He leaned back against the wall of the tunnel and closed his eyes. As he drifted into sleep, he heard the voices of the Shen in his head.

"You are doing well, Jack!"

"Prove yourself, Jack!"

"Not long now, Jack!"

In his dream, Jack saw the Shen swirl in front of him like brightly colored clouds. Then their voices changed.

"Rocks! Rocks! Rocks!"

It was Micah. Jack sprang awake, feeling slightly annoyed. Was that all the Terra could talk about?

But he could not see Micah.

"Rocks! Rocks!"

Tock was awake now, too. He and Jack ran toward the sound of Micah's voice.

"Micah!" Tock cried.

Jack and Tock stared at Micah. A strange creature held the small, screaming Terra above its head. The creature's body was made entirely of rocks. It had no eyes, nose, or mouth — just a smooth gray stone for a head.

Although it could not see, the creature seemed to sense Jack and Tock's presence. It turned around and seemed to stare at them with its blank face.

Then it hurled Micah into the air!

Jack leaped forward and caught Micah in his arms.

"Thanks," Micah said, hopping to the ground. His voice was shaking. "Should we throw rocks at it?"

The creature began to beat its chest with its arms in what looked like a fit of anger.

"I do not think that would help," Jack said.

The creature blocked their path, but it did not make a move toward them. Jack wanted to avoid attacking it if he could. It was probably just defending its home — but Jack didn't know how to tell it they did not mean any harm.

"This reminds me of a song I heard as a child," Tock

whispered. "Do you know it, Micah?"

Micah nodded. *"No eyes to see, no ears to hear, but if you move, you'd best beware,"* he said. "The song of the rock monster that lives deep within the mountain. I guess it wasn't just a child's tale."

Jack repeated the rhyme in his mind. *"If you move, you'd best beware."* Something clicked.

"The creature can feel the vibrations as we move through the tunnel," Jack guessed.

"That must be how he found me," Micah said. "I was throwing rocks against the wall to stay awake."

Tock frowned. "So if we stay perfectly still, he won't come after us?"

Jack nodded.

"Then we can't go on," Tock said.

"No," Jack said. "I know how to move so that no enemy can sense my coming."

"Let me guess," Tock said. "You'll carry us, right?"

Jack nodded again. Tock and Micah carefully picked up their packs. Then Jack grabbed one under each arm and moved forward. His years of samurai training had taught him to move like a ghost. He could bound across treetops without rustling a single leaf. He could race along the beach without leaving a print in the sand.

Sneaking past the rock monster should be easy.

Jack moved slowly and silently along the tunnel. The rock monster's blank face seemed to look right at them.

But it did not move toward them.

Jack could feel the Terras' hearts pounding in his

arms. He took another step closer to the monster. Now they were only inches away.

Jack turned sideways and slid along the wall. The space between him and the rock monster wasn't more than a few hairs wide. The rock monster grunted — but it did not sense them.

Jack took one final step past the monster. He heard Tock and Micah let out long relieved breaths. And then he heard —

Plink!

A small stone tumbled out of Micah's pack and landed on the floor. The monster turned toward them, swinging its rock-hard arm like a weapon.

Jack broke into a run and raced down the tunnel. The ground shook beneath them as the rock monster charged behind.

The tunnel made a sharp turn to the right. Jack followed it. Then he heard Tock yell, "Stop!"

The glowing bodies of the Terras illuminated a hole in

the wall leading to another tunnel. It was big enough for Jack — but too small for the rock monster.

Jack bent down. Tock and Micah scrambled through the hole. Jack followed.

The tunnel was just high enough for the Terras to walk upright. But Jack had to crouch down. A curious smell wafted toward them. Jack guessed there was an opening up ahead — but he did not know what they would find on the other side.

They did not have to wait long to find out. The tunnel opened up onto a small rock ledge. Tock and Micah gasped.

They were standing high on the wall of a huge cavern — almost as huge as the Terran city. But there was no beauty here.

Large mechanical roaches scuttled along the cavern floor. Each robot roach's back was covered with overlapping plates of silver metal. A red glass jewel shone on the middle of each roach's head.

Some of the roaches were digging tunnels into the

cavern walls. Others were emerging from the tunnels, carrying chunks of rock in their front legs. The rock was rust-red with streaks of silver-gray.

"What are they doing?" Micah asked.

"They are mining," Jack said. "Mining iron. For weapons." *For Aku,* Jack added to himself. Creatures like these could only have been created by Aku.

The roaches loaded the rocks into carts and dragged them through a tunnel — one that Jack guessed led outside the mountain.

In the center of the cavern was a large pool. The pool flowed into a stream that ran across the cavern and then headed underground. The once-clear water was streaked with rust and silver.

"Our water source," Tock said, with sadness in his voice. "The mining is leaking metals into our water."

"We've got to stop them!" Micah said. "Jack, what do we do?"

Jack put a hand on Micah's shoulder.

"Now," he said, "we throw rocks."

8

"Rocks?" Tock asked. "You've seen it yourself, Jack. These rocks aren't good for anything."

"Hey!" Micah protested.

Jack took a rock from Micah's pack.

"It is not the size of the rock," Jack said. "But where you aim it."

Jack hurled the rock down below. It smashed the jewel on the head of one of the robot roaches.

Electric sparks sizzled from the smashed jewel. The roach twitched violently, then collapsed to the ground. Thick gray smoke poured from its body.

It was just as Jack had guessed. The red jewel was the

source of the robot's power. Destroy the jewel, and the robot was powerless.

A horrible screeching sound rose up from the cavern. The heads of hundreds of robot roaches turned to look up the cavern wall at Jack, Tock, and Micah. Then the roaches began hurrying toward the wall. Some were climbing straight up toward the ledge that held them.

Micah threw a rock at one of the roaches. His aim was as good as Jack's. The roach screamed and tumbled back down the wall.

Tock and Micah should be able to hold off the robots for a while, Jack knew. But Micah's rocks would run out soon. Besides, Jack didn't need rocks.

He drew his sword.

"Good-bye, friends," he said. Before Tock or Micah could stop him, he leaped off the ledge.

Jack jumped from the back of one roach to another until he reached the cavern floor. Ten roaches immediately circled him, their front legs twitching.

Jack held his sword high, then spun around in a circle.

The sword's sharp blade chopped off the head of one robot after another. Seconds later, all ten robots collapsed.

Around him, Jack heard the sound of jewels cracking as Tock and Micah took down robot after robot. Jack concentrated on the robots on the floor. His sword ripped through metal again and again. But the more robots Jack destroyed, the more kept coming to attack him.

Only a small part of his brain thought about the huge numbers of attackers he faced. The rest of Jack's brain focused on destroying one robot at a time.

Slash! A robot tumbled to the ground.

Slash! Jack smashed the jewel of another robot.

Slash! Black oil spurted from a robot's neck as its head rolled off.

The robot roaches kept coming. They ignored Tock and Micah on their high perch and swarmed on Jack.

The Terras stared at the scene in horror. The center floor of the cavern was covered with crawling, screeching, robot roaches. Jack was nowhere to be seen.

"No!" Tock wailed.

And then, suddenly, a loud battle cry roared through the cavern. The pile of robot roaches began to shift.

Jack rose up from inside the pile, swinging his sword back and forth. His robes were torn. His face was streaked with dirt. But there was a look of determination on his face the Terras had not seen before.

Jack swung the sword with such force and speed that it looked like a blur of silver in the air. One by one, the remaining roaches fell to Jack's blade.

Sweat clouded Jack's eyes as the last robot roach fell

before him. He let out a deep breath and lowered his sword.

Plink!

Jack spun around. One last roach had crawled out of the pile and charged toward him. Now it lay on its back, the jewel in its head smashed to pieces.

"You're right, Jack!" Micah called down from the ledge. "It's all how you aim it!"

Tock was looking at his map.

"I think there's a way we can get down there," he said. "It's too high for us to jump."

"Stay where you are," Jack said. "I will come to you."

Jack sprung lightly across the bodies of the dead robots. He wondered what would happen next. Now that the robot mining operation had come to an end, the Terras' water should run clear in a week or so. He just had to help Tock and Micah get back home, and then he could finally reach the sage.

Suddenly, Jack felt the roaches rumble underneath his feet. A hot blast of wind singed his skin.

Jack turned around. The pool on the cavern floor bubbled like a pot of boiling water. The once-calm water was churning wildly.

A formless black shape began to rise out of the water like mist. The mist began to take form. A huge black body towered over the fallen roaches. A terrible green face took shape next. First, a green face mask. Then a mouth filled with sharp teeth. Red flames shot out above bulging white eyes.

"Aku!" Jack cried.

9

"Jack, why must you always hurt me?" Aku asked. His deep, sinister voice seemed to pierce Jack's skin.

Jack did not answer. He stood, poised to attack at a moment's notice. He gripped his sword tightly and held it out in front of him.

Aku feared the sword, he knew. It was Jack's father's sword, the only instrument capable of harming Aku. The sword was the main reason that Jack was alive. Aku did not like to fight Jack while the samurai held the sword. He preferred to let others do it for him.

Aku opened his mouth to speak. But before he could, a small rock sailed past his face. Startled, Aku turned toward the ledge that held the Terras. Micah held another rock in his hand, ready to throw again.

Jack tried not to show his fear. The demon turned back to Jack and grinned. It was the kind of grin that makes you wish you were far away from the person grinning.

"Yes, Jack, I will not fight you while you hold the sword," Aku said. "But I can hurt those who aid you."

The Terras watched, frozen in fear, as Aku transformed into a giant cockroach. He was ten times bigger than his robot workers — and ten times more sinister-looking. Razor-sharp spikes protruded from his front legs.

Aku scuttled up the cavern wall, headed right toward Tock and Micah. Jack tucked the sword in his belt and jumped over the fallen robots. Above him, he saw Aku swipe at the Terras. Tock and Micah moved to avoid the spikes — and went tumbling off of the ledge!

Jack jumped as high and hard as he ever had, catching the two Terras in his arms. Above him, Aku gave an angry roar.

Jack jumped again, landing next to one of the tunnels the robots had dug. He set Tock and Micah on the ground.

"Run," he told them.

"No, Jack!" Micah said. "We will help you."

"Please," Jack said. "I must do this alone."

Tock understood. He grabbed Micah by the arm. "The Terras will never forget you, Jack. We will make sure of that."

Tock and Micah turned and vanished into the tunnel. There was no time for Jack to say good-bye to his new friends. He turned, drew his sword, and faced Aku.

"*Aaaaaaaaaaah!*" Jack cried, charging toward the demon. He swung his sword at Aku with all his might.

Aku moved swiftly on his six insect legs, dodging the blow. He raced across the canyon and climbed on top of the pile of fallen robots.

"Have you learned nothing, Samurai?" Aku taunted. "You cannot destroy me!"

Aku hissed, and a spray of foul-smelling green liquid flew from his mouth. Jack dodged out of the way just in time. He heard the liquid sizzle as it hit the rocks behind him.

"This ends now," Jack said firmly. He charged ahead once more, jumping on top of the robot pile.

Two black wings opened up on Aku's back. The demon flew away, landing on a heap of boulders.

"Your little friend likes to throw rocks," Aku said. "I can throw rocks, too!"

Aku grabbed one of the boulders in his front legs. He hurled the boulder at Jack.

Jack heard the boulder whiz past his ear as he leaped to the side. The boulder thudded onto the cavern floor.

More boulders flew toward him at a furious pace. There was no time to look for cover.

Woosh! Jack dodged to the left.

Woosh! Jack dodged to the right.

Woosh! Jack somersaulted as a boulder flew just inches over his head.

All the while, Jack did not take his eyes off of Aku. The demon could not throw boulders forever. And Jack had something better than boulders.

He had his sword.

Aku frowned as another boulder missed Jack by a hair. The demon paused for a second. Then he smiled. He shape-shifted again, until he grew another ten feet. He picked up a huge boulder, twice as big as any he had thrown.

Then he changed his aim. This time, Aku aimed the boulder at the pile of robots under Jack's feet.

It only took a second for Jack to realize what the

demon was trying to do. He tried to leap into the air, but the boulder hit too fast. The pile of roaches collapsed, sending Jack cascading toward the stream.

Jack landed on the ground with a loud thud. The force sent the sword flying out of his hands. It landed in the stream, and the swiftly moving water carried it away.

Jack scrambled toward the water, but Aku appeared, blocking his way. The demon had shape-shifted again. Now he was a giant black spider.

"Not so fast, Samurai," Aku cackled.

Sticky strands of webbing flew out of Aku's mouth and wrapped around Jack's body. Jack struggled to get out of his binds, but it was no use. The strong strands could not be broken.

Aku crouched down on his eight legs. The demon's face hovered inches above Jack's. The samurai could smell his hot, foul breath.

Aku grinned, exposing two long, sharp spider fangs.

"Now, foolish Samurai," Aku said, "we finish this."

10

"*Jack has proved himself.*"

"*Jack is a friend.*"

"*You are our enemy.*"

The voices of the Shen echoed throughout the cavern. Brilliant streaks of blue, green, and gold light swirled around them.

"Who dares to interrupt Aku?" the demon bellowed.

But the voices of the Shen drowned out Aku's cries. Jack watched as the swirling light surrounded the demon.

Aku vanished.

Before Jack could blink, the swirling lights surround-

ed him, too. In the next instant, he found himself outside. He was free of the sticky spiderwebs. His robe was white and clean, as though nothing had happened.

Once again the Shen Mountains towered above Jack. He shielded his eyes from the bright sunlight. Something glittered on the ground in front of him.

His sword! Jack picked it up and returned it to his belt.

"Good work, Jack!" a familiar voice cackled.

The raven was perched on the branch of a nearby tree.

"So this was a test?" Jack asked, walking toward it.

The raven's head bobbed up and down. "You are a friend!"

It all began to sink in. He had lost the talisman given to him by the monks, so the Shen did not know if they could trust him. They must have led him to the Terras to see if he would help them. When he proved himself, the Shen had saved him from Aku.

"Tock and Micah?" Jack asked.

"They are back in the Terran city," the raven said.

"And Aku?"

The raven ruffled its black feathers. *"Caw!* Aku is gone from the Shen Mountains," he said. "But not destroyed."

Jack had guessed as much. But he had one last question.

"I entered the mountains in search of a sage," he said. "Do you know where I can find him?"

"You have crossed the mountain," the raven said. "The Shen have brought you here. What you seek lies beyond those trees."

The raven moved its head toward the valley beyond. It was not like the valley on the other side of the mountain, which was bleak and bare. Green grass stretched out before them. Rising up from the green was a stand of tall trees. The sage must be on the other side.

"Thank you," Jack said.

The raven nodded. "You are a friend, Jack. You may pass through the Shen Mountains at any time."

And then, as Jack watched, the raven's body began to swirl with color. The colors broke apart into blue, green, and gold, and suddenly the woman, old man, and young boy of the Shen floated before him.

"Good-bye, Jack."

"You are worthy, Jack."

"Don't give up!"

Jack gave the Shen a respectful bow. Then he walked across the grass toward the trees. He soon came to a stream and took a long, cool drink.

Another person might have run through those trees, trembling with excitement. But Jack had been close to his goal many times before — only to see it dissolve before him. So he walked on steadily, ready for whatever might happen.

Overhead, the leaves of the trees shimmered in the sunlight. Then the sun grew brighter, and Jack stepped out from beneath the last tree.

A small hill rose up in front of him. On top of the hill sat a little cabin made of logs.

Above the door was a circle of wood with a black bird painted on it.

A raven.

Jack knew he had found the right place. He walked up the hill and opened the door.

Sunlight streamed through the back wall of the cabin, which looked as though it had been knocked down by a battering ram. The crude furniture in the cabin was broken and strewn around the room. There was no sign of the sage anywhere.

Jack searched through the rubble. Something shiny and red caught his eye. He picked it up. It was a jewel from one of Aku's robot insects.

Jack sighed. The robots must have destroyed the

cabin weeks ago — probably on Aku's orders. All was lost.

Or was it? The cabin was destroyed, that was true. But there was no sign that the sage had been harmed.

The sage was alive, and out there somewhere.

And somewhere deep inside Jack, hope sparked once again.

Jack stepped outside the cabin and looked up at the Shen Mountains.

"I will not give up," he said quietly. Then he walked off into the valley.

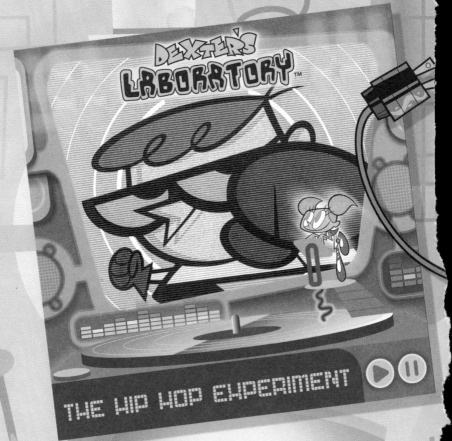